To New York

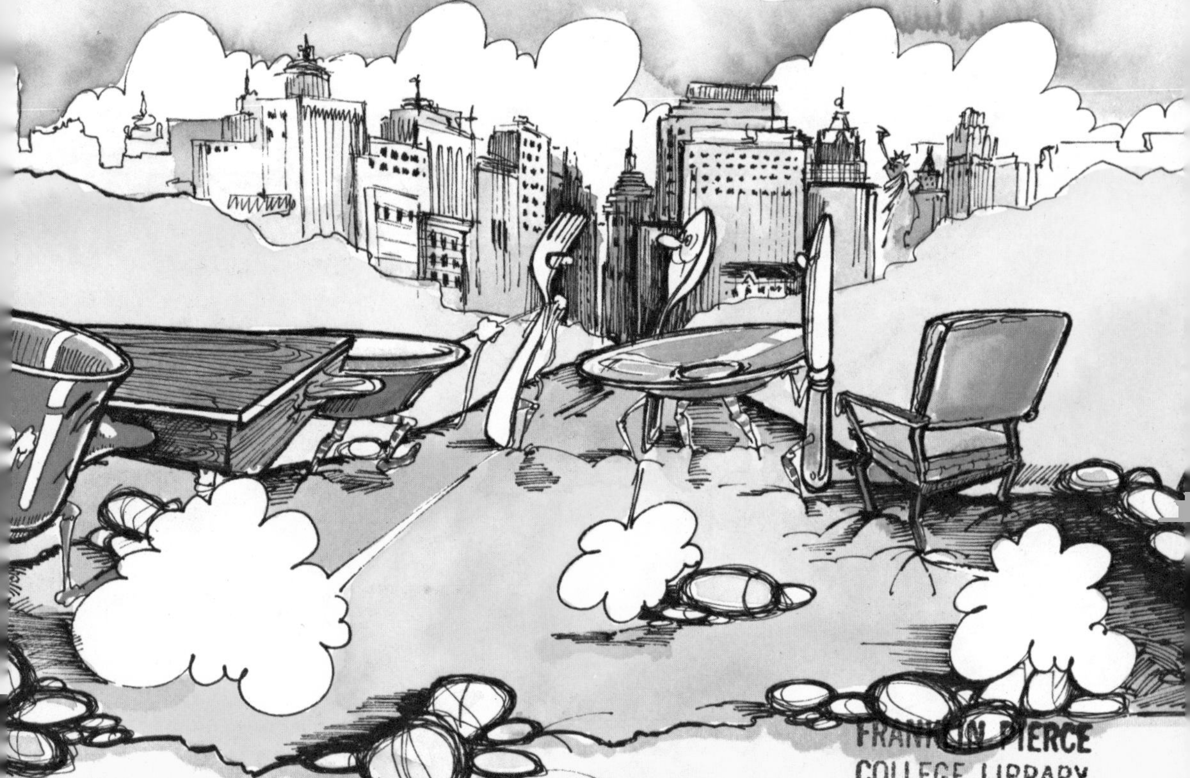

by June Melser

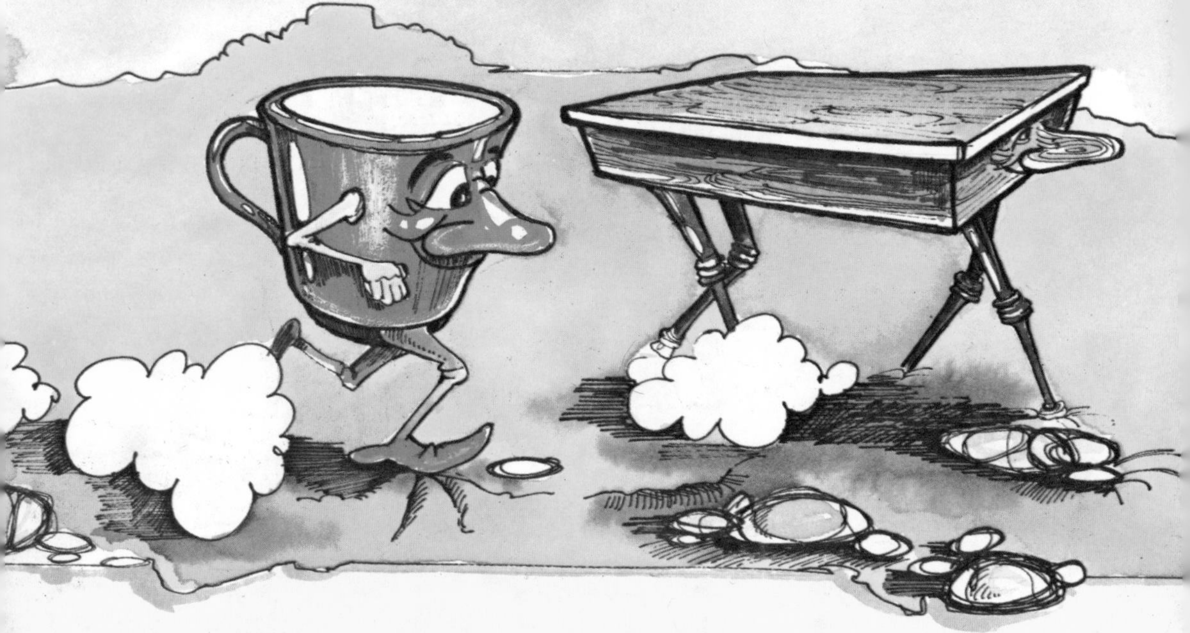

The cup, the table,

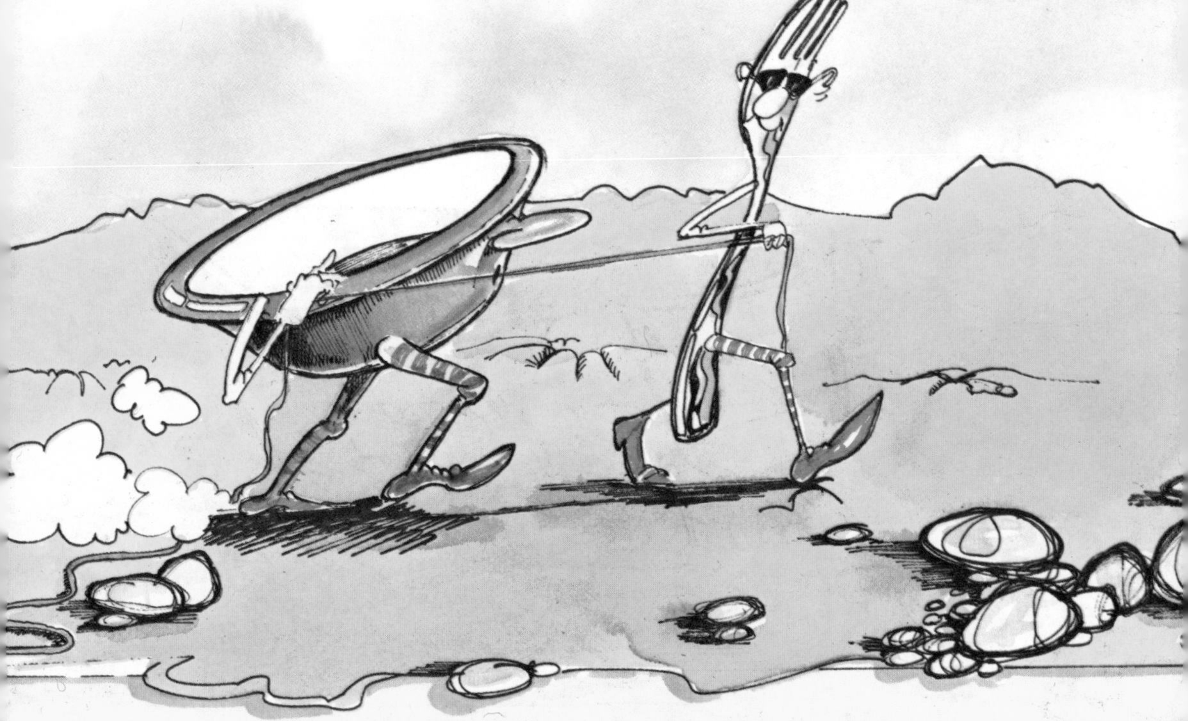

the dish, the fork

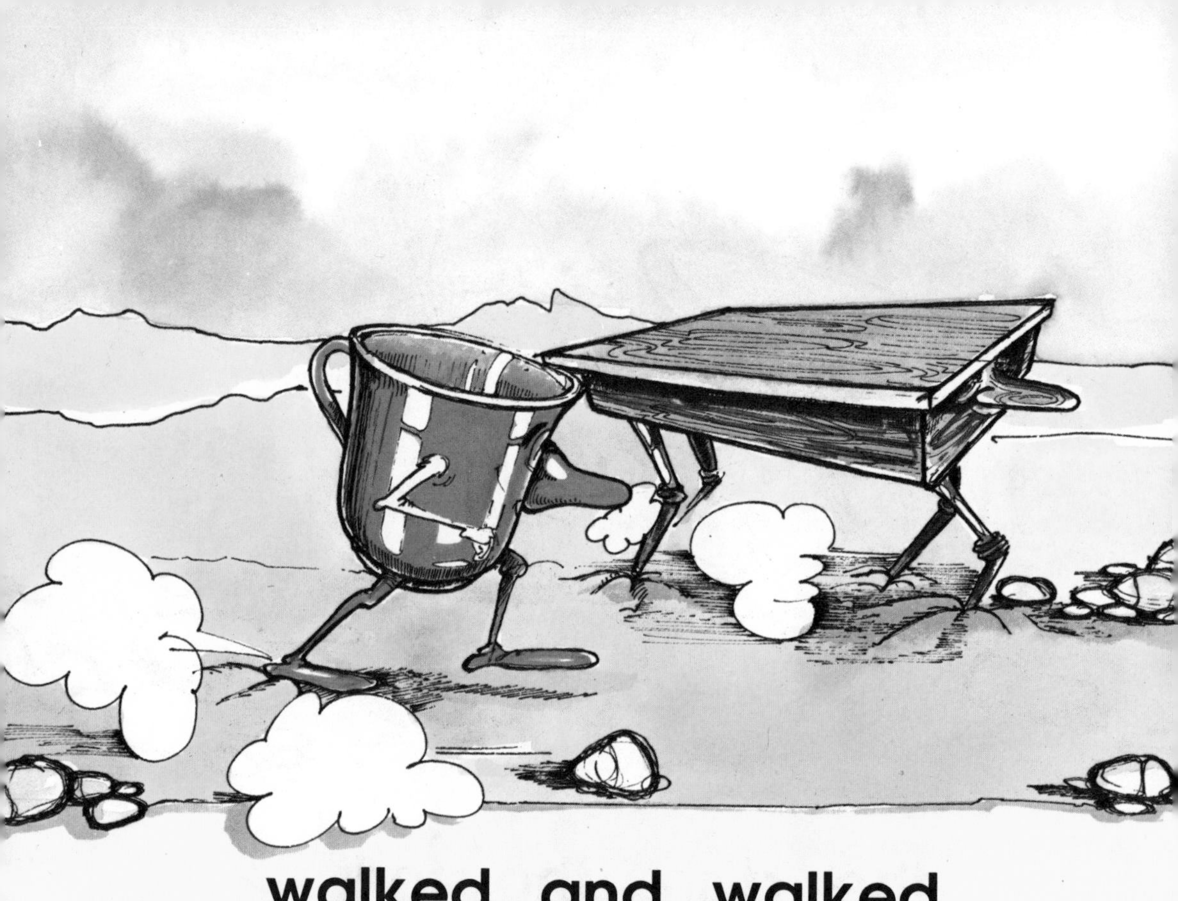

walked and walked

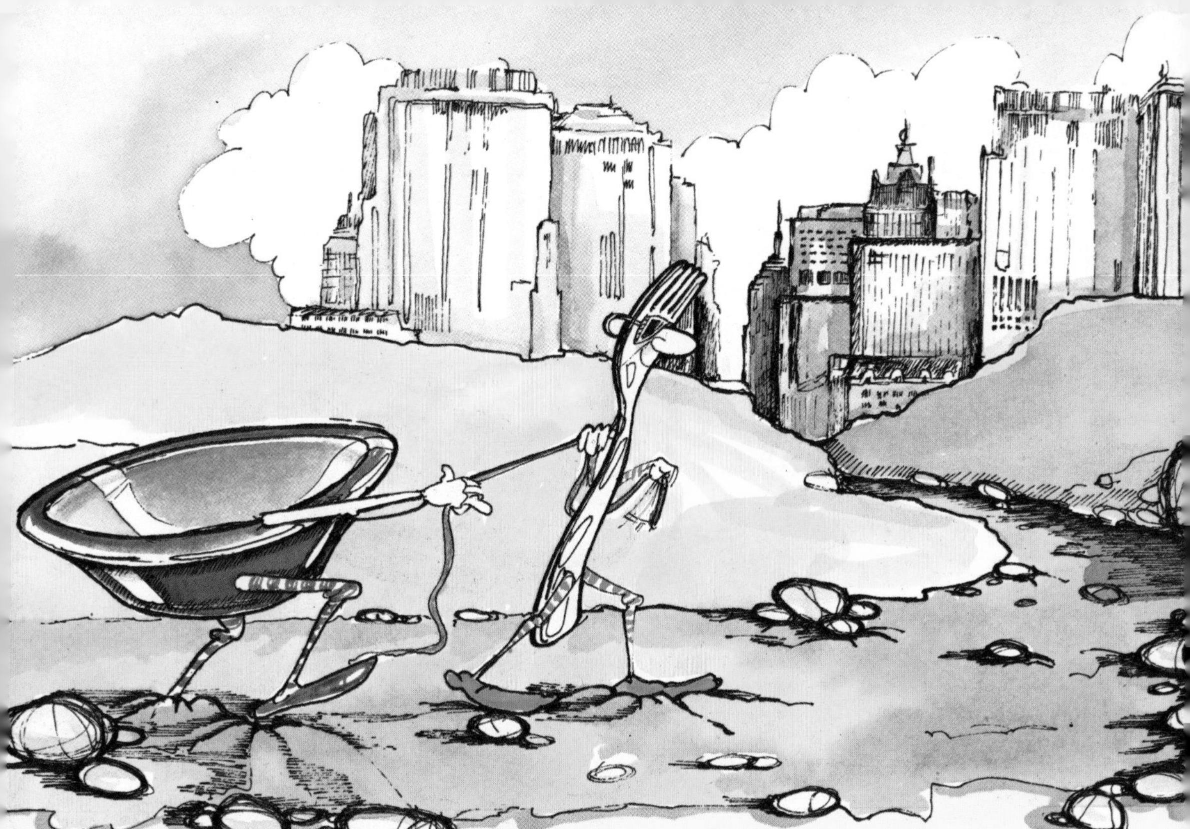

all the way to New York.

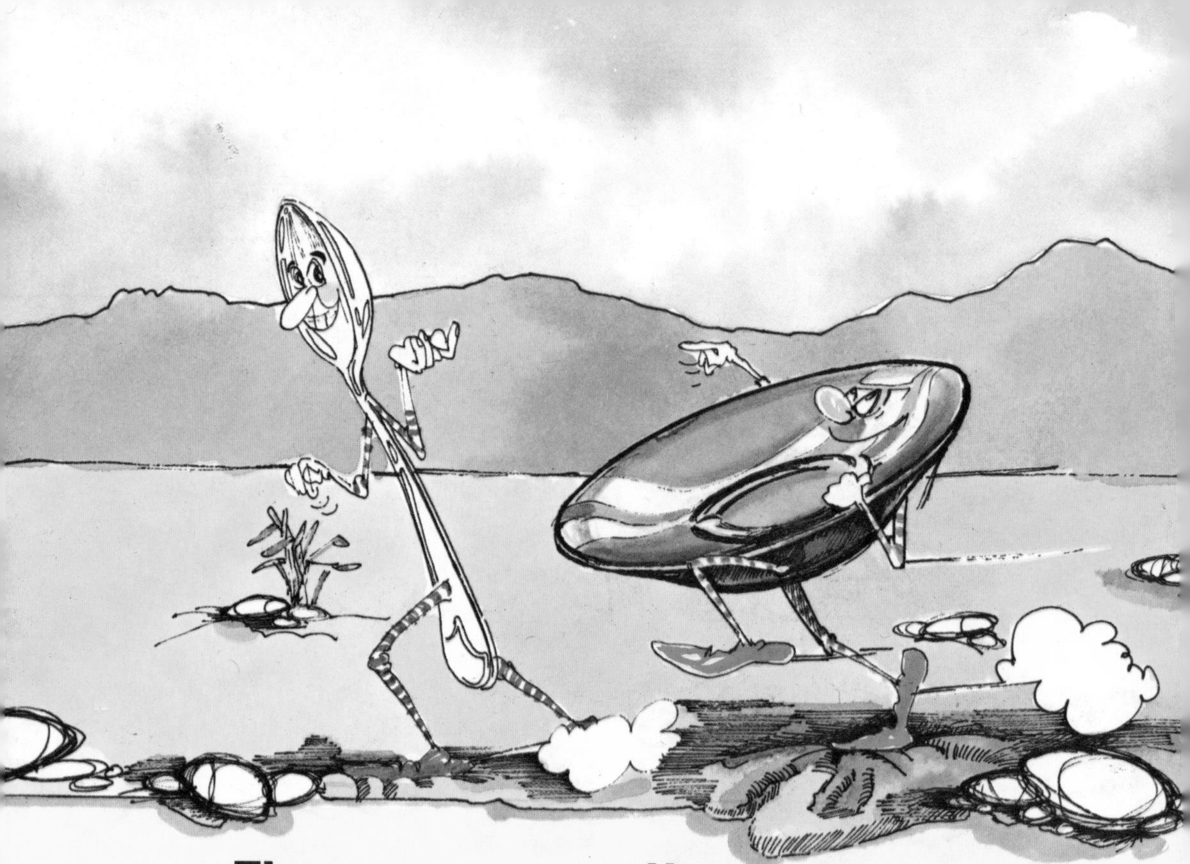

The spoon, the saucer,

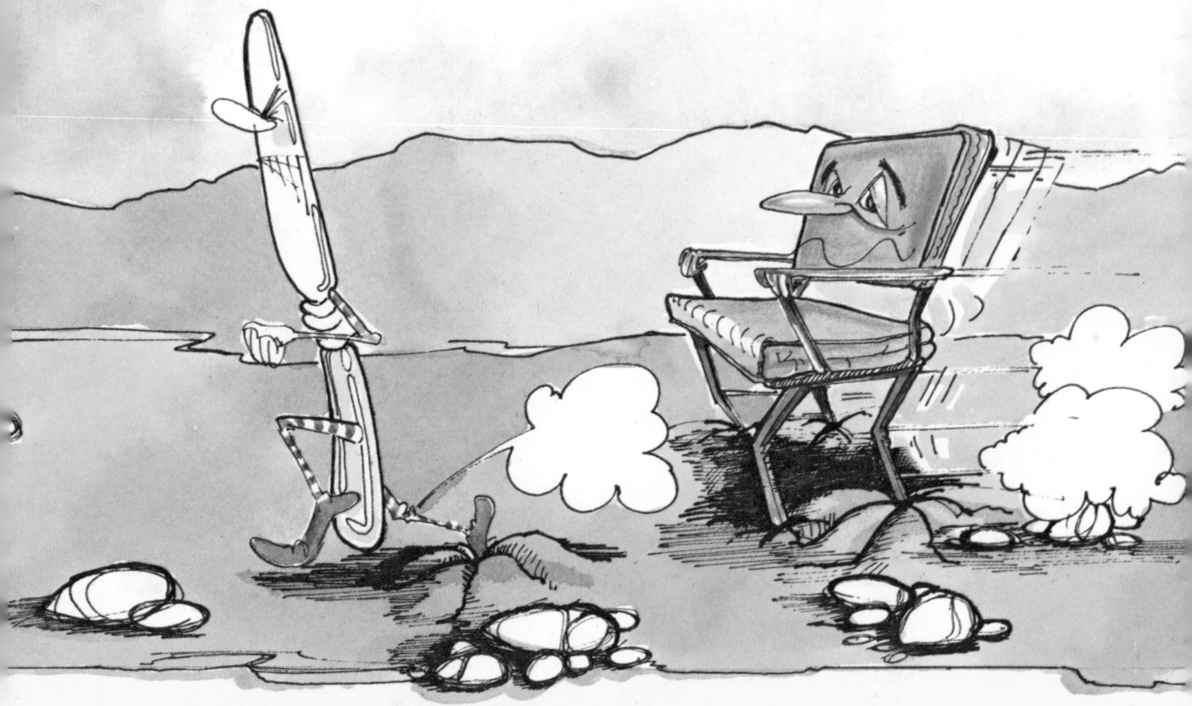

the knife, the chair

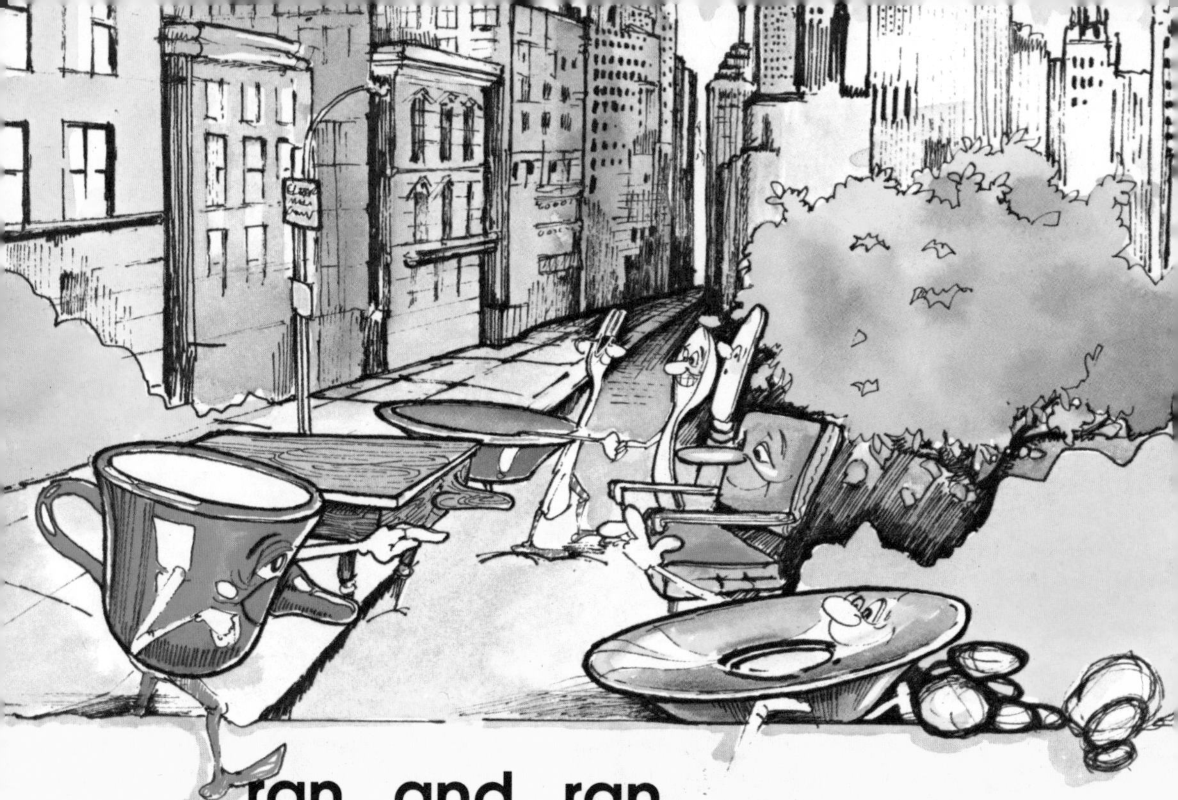

ran and ran
and met them there.